D1457818

I CAN READ ABOUT

MAGELLAN

Written by Darrow Schecter

Illustrated by Herb Mott

Troll Associates

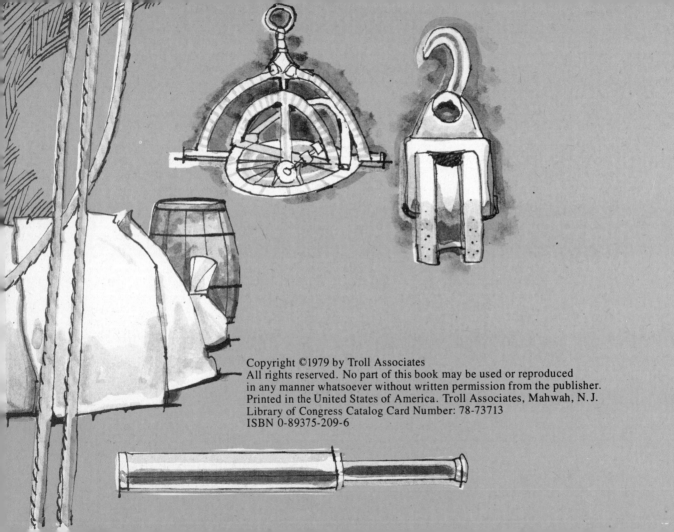

A long time ago,
people did not know
what the world was like.

There were unknown seas,
and oceans, and strange lands.
Some people even believed
in sea monsters.

Then, in 1492, a man named Christopher Columbus discovered a new continent. Christopher Columbus thought he was near India. But he was wrong.

Still...when people heard about Christopher Columbus' discovery, they were eager to know more. The countries of Europe—especially Spain and Portugal—wanted to learn about new lands and places. They were eager for riches and adventure!

OCEAN

PORTUGAL

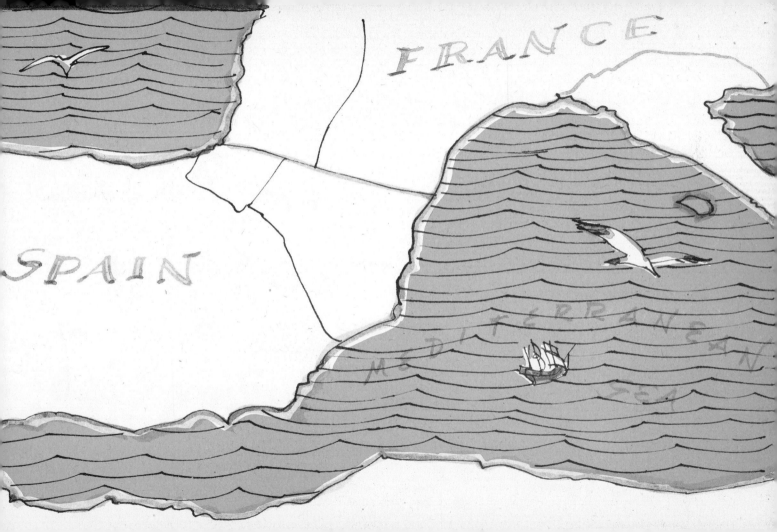

This is the story of one explorer.
In his search for riches and adventure,
he *proved* that the world was round.
His name was Ferdinand Magellan.

Ferdinand Magellan grew up in northern Portugal. When he was a young boy, his life was happy.

Then, when he was about 12,
he was sent to Lisbon. He went
to the Queen's court to become a page.
    As a page, Ferdinand was taught
good manners. He met famous people,
and got to know the poets, artists and
wise people of the city.

At first Ferdinand was sad to leave home. His home town was small and quiet. Lisbon was noisy and crowded.

But it was in Lisbon that Ferdinand Magellan first set eyes on the ocean. What a sight it was!

Ferdinand Magellan watched the ships in the harbor. The ships carried silks and spices from India. The wonderful sights he saw made him dream of adventure.

He decided to learn more. He mastered geography and navigation. He began to wonder if the world was larger than most people thought.

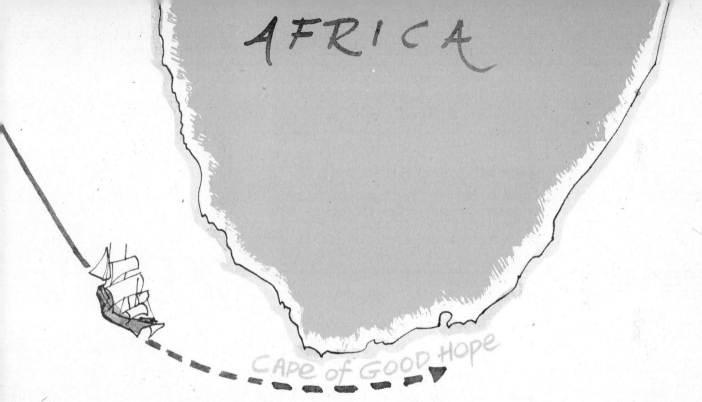

AFRICA

Cape of Good Hope

Several years before, an explorer named Bartholomew Dias had sailed to the tip of Africa—to the Cape of Good Hope. This was as far as ships had gone. Magellan now wondered what was beyond the tip of Africa.

He was especially interested
in trade routes.
Magellan was curious about the
routes that led to India.
What was beyond India?

When he was 19, Magellan learned that Vasco da Gama had sailed around the Cape of Good Hope. Then Vasco da Gama had sailed across an unknown ocean and reached India by water. This made Magellan even more eager to explore new lands. He, too, wanted to go on these voyages of discovery.

In 1505, Magellan got his chance.
He went with a fleet that was sailing to India, and beyond.

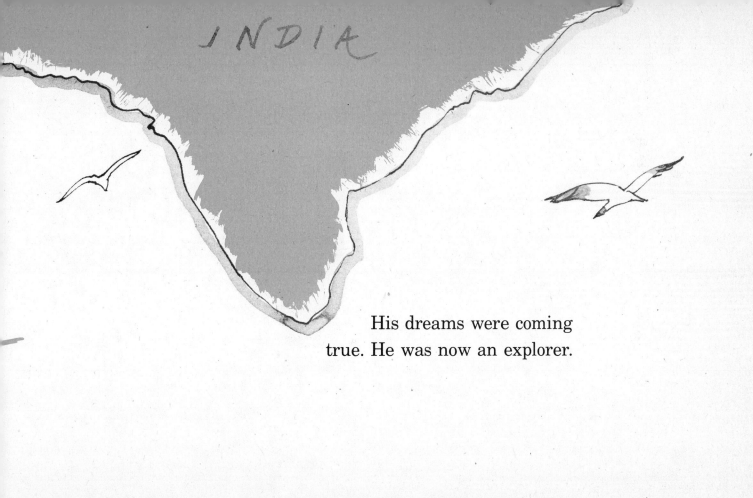

His dreams were coming
true. He was now an explorer.

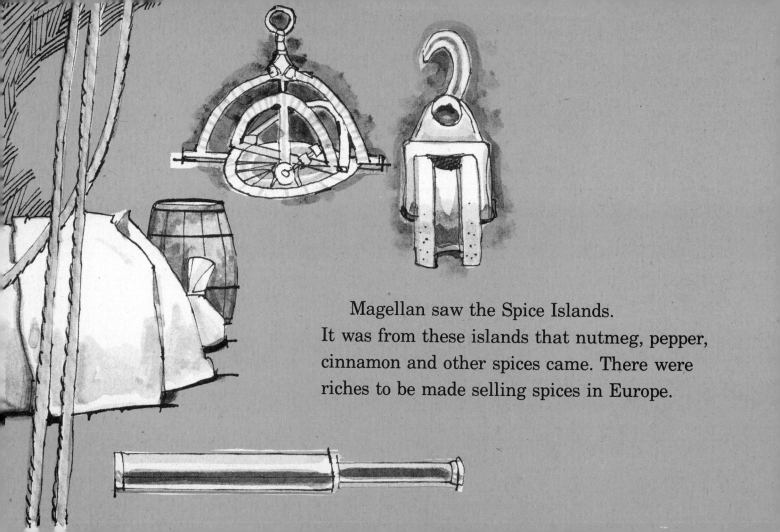

Magellan saw the Spice Islands.
It was from these islands that nutmeg, pepper,
cinnamon and other spices came. There were
riches to be made selling spices in Europe.

Magellan was sure that beyond
the Spice Islands there was still
another ocean. So he secretly
explored the area by ship.

MALAY PENINSULA

MALAYSIA

MALACCA

SINGAPORE

SUMATRA

JAKARTA

JAVA

BORNEO

CELEBES

PHILIPPINE ISLANDS

MOLUCCA SEA

SPICE ISLANDS

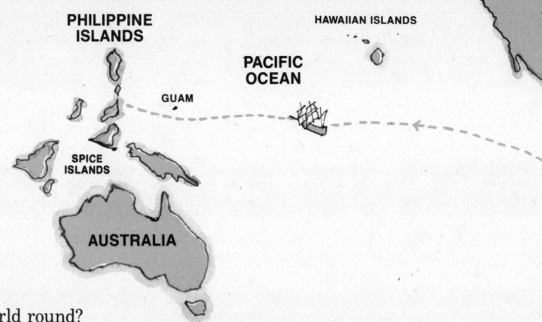

Was the world round?
Magellan had an idea. Like Columbus before him,
Magellan believed he could reach the East and the Spice Islands
by sailing west. He *knew* his idea would work.

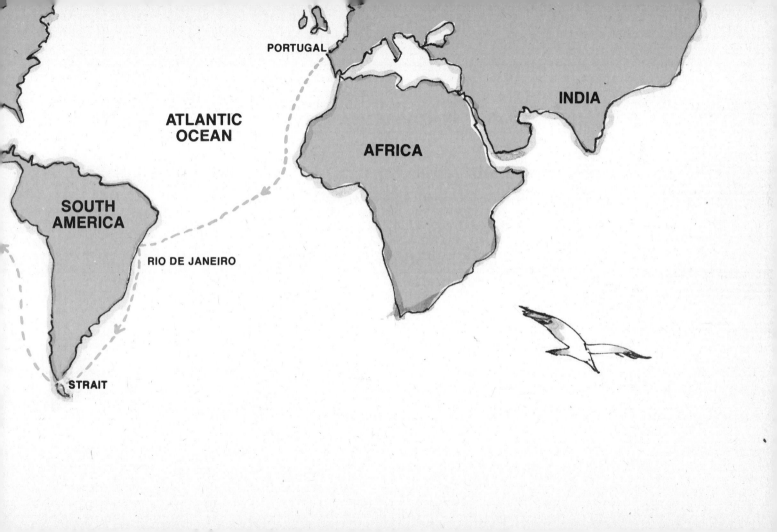

PORTUGAL

ATLANTIC
OCEAN

AFRICA

INDIA

SOUTH
AMERICA

RIO DE JANEIRO

STRAIT

Now he needed money and ships.
First he went to the King of Portugal.
Then, in 1517, he went to the
King of Spain. The King of Spain
was interested in Magellan's
idea of sailing westward around
the earth. The king hoped Magellan
would discover new lands
and new riches.

In the year 1519, Magellan left Spain
with a fleet of five ships and 240 sailors.
His ship was called the *Trinidad*.
The other ships were the *Santiago*,
the *San Antonio*, the *Concepción*,
and the *Victoria*.

The trip across the Atlantic
was long and dangerous. When the ships
reached South America, they continued south
and entered a bay near Rio de Janeiro.
The trip had taken almost three months.

Then the ships continued on. They were looking for a passageway, or strait, through the land which would take them to the other side. Magellan studied his maps carefully.

Mutiny broke out on three of the ships.
When it was over, Magellan took control again.
But gale winds smashed and wrecked
the *Santiago*.

Later the men went ashore. They hunted birds, caught fish, and made winter clothes from sealskins. They smoked the fish and put them in barrels for the voyage at sea.

They sailed on, always watching for a passageway.
Then one day it happened! A terrible
wind drove the *San Antonio* and the
Concepción clear through to the
other side—to the Great South Sea—
the Pacific Ocean. The passageway
was found—thanks to the wind.
The passageway would be called
the Strait of Magellan.

The ships headed into unknown waters. "Steer west to the Spice Islands," cried Magellan. But the captain of the *San Antonio* secretly turned back and headed for Spain.

The remaining ships sailed
for three months on the Pacific Ocean
without seeing land. Day by day,
the burning sun baked their bodies.

Fresh drinking water was now gone.
The little food left in the barrels
was crawling with worms. The
sailors were starving and ate
leather and sawdust to fill
their empty stomachs.
Death and disease followed
the ships.

Suddenly, on January 24, 1521, land was sighted and Magellan's crew went ashore. There were birds, and turtle eggs, and even sharks to catch.

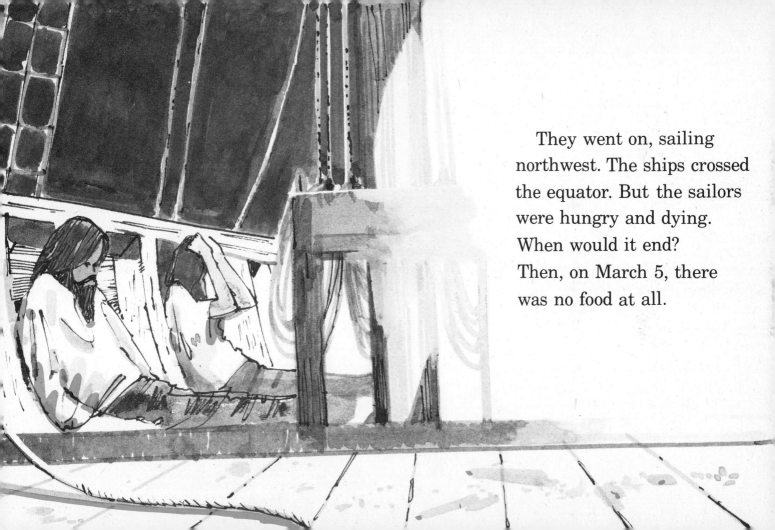

They went on, sailing
northwest. The ships crossed
the equator. But the sailors
were hungry and dying.
When would it end?
Then, on March 5, there
was no food at all.

Suddenly, they sighted land. It was an unknown island—Guam—near the Philippines. But a battle broke out between the islanders and Magellan's sailors. The crew took what food they could and fled.

They continued on to the Philippine Islands.
They had been out on the Pacific for three months and
twenty days.
Magellan was not far from the Spice Islands.

But death was waiting for him. He would never reach
the Spice Islands.

In the Philippines, Magellan believed it was his duty
to teach the islanders his religion. In his efforts
to help an island ruler, Magellan was killed on the island
of Mactan. As his men fled to their boats, they left
Magellan dead on the shore.

The *Concepción* was burned. Not enough sailors were left to fill the ship. The two remaining ships sailed on to the Spice Islands. Later, the *Trinidad* was captured by the Portuguese.

Finally, in 1522, almost three years later, the *Victoria* returned to Spain. The boat had gone around the world. Only 18 men were left. They were barefoot and ill and were happy just to be alive. But they proved that this voyage was more than a dream. This voyage was one of the great adventures in discovery. They proved it could be done.